For my best boy in the whole world, Sam — N.W.

For Julius — M.J.

Published in Canada by Tundra Books,
a division of Random House of Canada Limited,
One Toronto Street, Suite 300, Toronto, Ontario M5C 2V6

Published in the United States by Tundra Books of Northern New York,
P.O. Box 1030, Plattsburgh, New York 12901

Library of Congress Control Number: 2014941836

www.tundrabooks.com

Library and Archives Canada Cataloguing in Publication

Winstanley, Nicola, author
    The pirate's bed / Nicola Winstanley ; illustrated by Matt James.

Issued in print and electronic formats.
ISBN 978-1-77049-616-3 (bound).—ISBN 978-1-77049-618-7 (epub)

    I. James, Matt, 1973–, illustrator II. Title.

PS8645.I57278P57 2015   jC813'.6   C2014-903059-2
                                     C2014-903060-6

Edited by Samantha Swenson
Designed by Leah Springate
The artwork in this book was rendered in acrylic paint and India ink on board.

Printed and bound in China

1 2 3 4 5 6   20 19 18 17 16 15

THE PIRATE'S BED

NICOLA WINSTANLEY

ILLUSTRATED BY MATT JAMES

A great storm came up at sea.

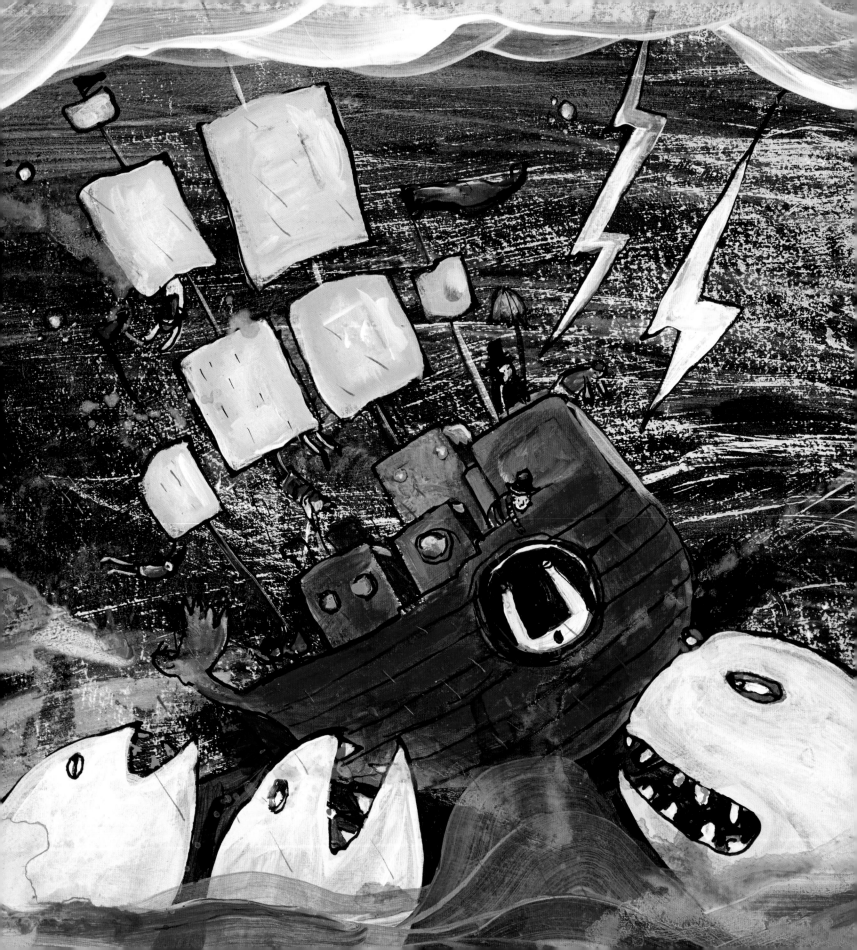

The pirate ship pitched and rolled. With every rising wave, the pirate's bed slid across the cabin floor and back again as the wave came down.

Every downward swoosh was faster and deeper than the one before.

The bed skittered across the floor, afraid. But the pirate slept on, rocked like a baby in a cradle.

The pirate snored and dreamed comfortable pirate dreams of sitting aloft in the crow's nest at dawn. He dreamed of pirate adventures too—of long treks through dense jungle, his yo-ho-hos ringing in the steamy air. He dreamed of the wondrous things he had seen: monkeys chattering in coconut palms, snakes as thick as tree trunks, giant waterfalls and pools of hot bubbling mud.

He had been a long time at sea. He had slept many nights curled
up with his cutlass in the small bed, dreaming and snoring. Being
a pirate was tiring work. He had slept through many storms,
lulled by the creaking of the boat, the howl of the wind and the
roar of the ocean.

But the bed was wide awake and not so comfortable. It knew this storm was a wild one, unlike any other.

And sure enough, the bed slid once more as a single wave, like a wall of water, lifted the ship and crashed it upon the rocks. The pirate and all his shipmates fell into the sea, and the waves carried them to the shores of an island.

They lived in peace for the
rest of their days, eating
sweet fruit and teaching
parrots to talk.

But the pirate's bed was not so fortunate.
All alone, it was swept in another direction
altogether. Far, far away.

When the storm was finally spent, the bed bobbed on
the calm ocean like a small vessel, the straw mattress and
woolen blanket gone. It was a sturdy bed, and sensible.
It knew there was nothing to do but wait and see.

The bed floated for many days, pulled this way and that
by deep undersea currents.

For some time, the bed was very happy in its new life.
The pirate was fat and heavy and had never changed
his socks; his snoring had shaken the hull of the
ship and rattled everything in the cabin. The straw
mattress had been scratchy and full of fleas and other
bugs. The bed had wondered, then, what it would be
like to be free of the pirate's hulking sleeping body.

Now it knew! Every day the sun shone bright and warm
in the enormous blue sky, and birds would appear
as if from nowhere to rest on the frame and preen
themselves. The bed liked the company, and didn't mind
the feel of the birds' sharp claws. Once, a large gull
stood on the headboard and stretched its wings wide.
And the bed, with its new sail, sped across the open
water, laughing.

One morning, a school of playful dolphins swam around the little bed, nudging it. The bed joined them in their game and dipped and bobbed joyfully at their prodding. When the dolphins sliced the air with their silvery, sickle-shaped bodies, the bed thought it had never seen such a beautiful sight.

Day after day, the sun shone, the birds chattered and flapped, and the sea sighed gently. But as the bed drifted across the water, its happiness was drifting further and further away.

It wasn't only that the bed couldn't leap and swim like a dolphin. Or fly away to land, like a bird. The bed knew that something was missing.

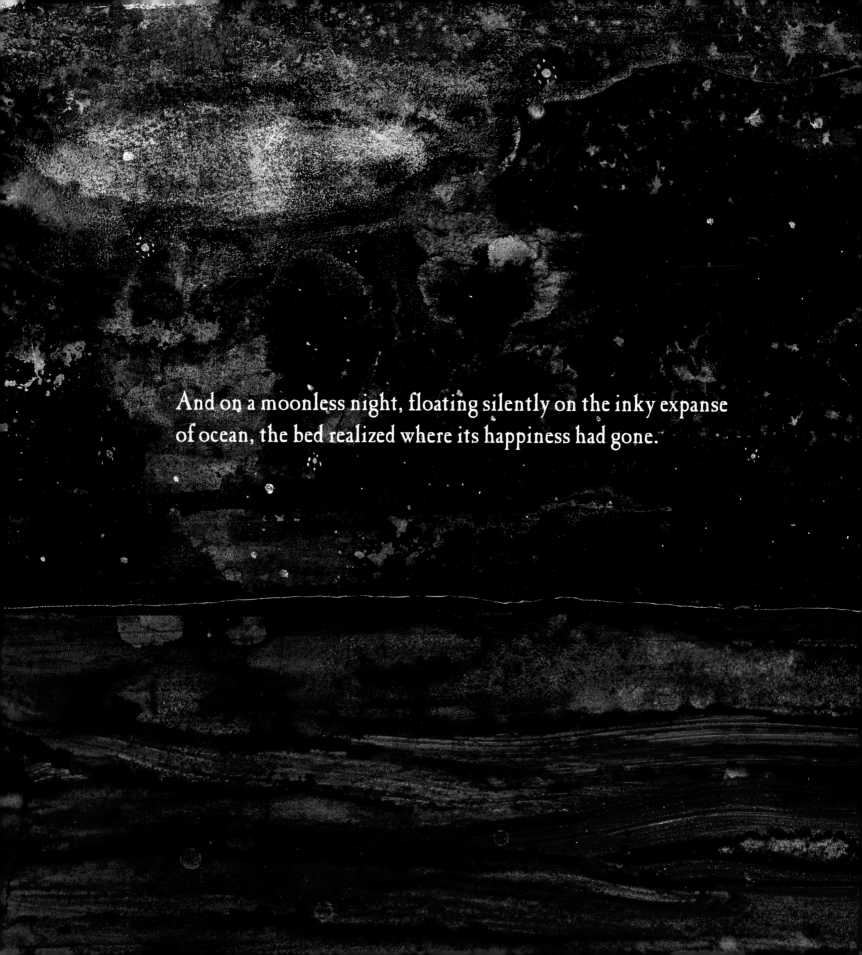

And on a moonless night, floating silently on the inky expanse of ocean, the bed realized where its happiness had gone.

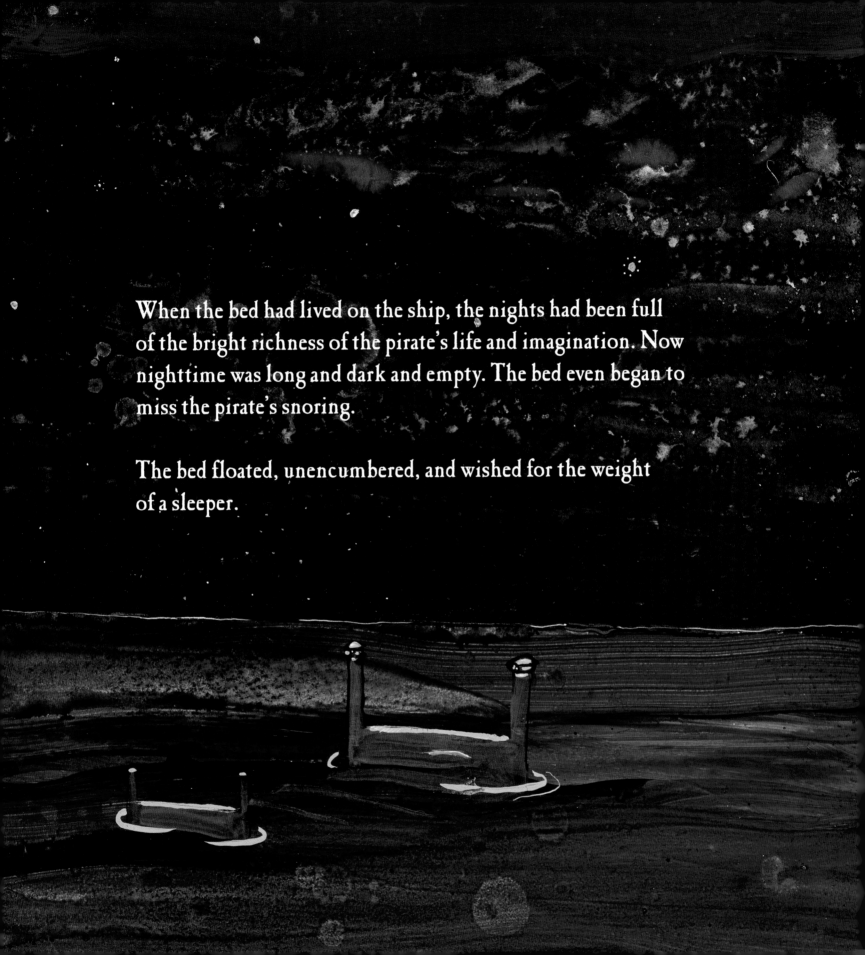

When the bed had lived on the ship, the nights had been full
of the bright richness of the pirate's life and imagination. Now
nighttime was long and dark and empty. The bed even began to
miss the pirate's snoring.

The bed floated, unencumbered, and wished for the weight
of a sleeper.

Luckily the sea has a way of bringing things to shore. And, after many dreamless, lonely nights, the bed, now battered and swollen, felt land beneath it. It saw that it had been gently pushed onto a sandy beach.

A carpenter found the little bed and liked the look of its sturdy frame. He took it home, dried it out and cleaned the wood of seaweed and salt. When it was ready, the carpenter put the bed in his shop for sale. At last, the bed was clean and warm and dry. And it waited, patient and hopeful.

One day, at last, a young mother came into the shop. When she saw the tidy bed, she knew it would be just right for her little boy.

She brought it home and told him that the bed was found washed up on the beach.

"A pirate's bed!" the boy exclaimed. He knew all about pirates, and loved them too. "A pirate's bed knows where the treasure is buried!" he told her. "The pirate tells his pillow where X marks the spot, and only the bed knows." The little bed smiled inside. It knew. It did.

"Maybe," the mother said when she tucked him in, "you'll dream some pirate dreams in your pirate bed."

And as soon as the little boy snuggled down under the covers and closed his eyes, he felt the whooshing and swooshing of waves and smelt the briny smell of the sea. The hot sun beat down on his large brimmed hat. Parrots squawked and raucous pirates sang raucous pirate songs. The boy breathed in the tangy scent of pineapples and passion fruit.

And as the bed breathed in with him, it found that happiness had finally returned.

Many years later, the little boy became a father, and he gave the bed to his own little boy. As time went on, the bed was passed from family to family. And whoever slept in that square-framed, solid and sensible bed felt the rock of the ocean on dry land.

It might be that the bed was passed down to you!

Perhaps you sleep in it now. Perhaps you dream of parrots flying over white sand, of sails full of wind, of long-buried treasure. (Perhaps, if you listen carefully, the bed will tell you where the treasure is buried . . .)

But if you don't? Then you can dream your own dreams and keep your own bed company through the night. And it will comfort you, keep you warm, and thank you for changing your socks and not shaking the walls when you snore.